First Facts®

Expert Pet Care

CARING for Hermit Crabs

A 4D BOOK

by Tammy Gagne

Consultant:
Jennifer Zablotny, DVM
Member, American Veterinary Medical Association

PEBBLE
a capstone imprint

Download the Capstone app!

- Ask an adult to download the Capstone 4D app.

- Scan the cover and stars inside the book for additional content.

When you scan a spread, you'll find fun extra stuff to go with this book! You can also find these things on the web at www.capstone4D.com using the password: hermitcrabs.27421

First Facts are published by Pebble
1710 Roe Crest Drive, North Mankato, Minnesota 56003
www.mycapstone.com

Library of Congress Cataloging-in-Publication Data
is available on the Library of Congress website.

ISBN 978-1-5435-2742-1 (library binding)
ISBN 978-1-5435-2748-3 (paperback)
ISBN 978-1-5435-2754-4 (ebook pdf)

Editorial Credits
Marissa Kirkman, editor; Sarah Bennett, designer; Tracy Cummins, media researcher; Laura Manthe, production specialist

Photo Credits
Capstone Studio: Karon Dubke, 6, 7, 10, 11, 13, 15, 16, 17, 19; Shutterstock: Andrew Burgess, 23, davemhuntphotography, 21 Top, ekmelica, Design Element, Eric Isselee, Cover Back, 3, Guillermo Guerao Serra, 21 Middle, Jose Gil, 21 Bottom Left, MR.Yanukit, 5, Oliver Foerstner, 21 Bottom Right, Physics_joe, 18, qingqing, 24, Sukanin18, 9 Top, 20, Victor Shova, 9 Bottom, Wow Pho, Cover.

Printed in the United States of America.
PA017

Table of Contents

Your New Pet Hermit Crabs

Most crabs live near the beach and would not be good pets. But a hermit crab can live safely in your home. It is important to know how to care for one before buying it.

You can find hermit crabs at many pet stores. These pets do best when kept in groups. You should get three or more crabs as pets.

FACT

Different kinds of hermit crabs can live in a group. Ask a worker at the pet store to help you pick a group of crabs.

Supplies You Will Need

A covered **aquarium** is a great new home for your hermit crabs. The tank size depends on how many crabs you have.

You'll need to get food, water, sand, a heater, and a **thermometer**. Your crabs also need climbing toys and extra shells. These animals move from one shell to another during their lives. You will need at least three shells per crab in the tank at all times. This will keep crabs from fighting over them.

aquarium—a glass tank where pets, including
hamsters, hermit crabs, and fish, are kept

thermometer—a tool that measures temperature

Bringing Your Hermit Crabs Home

Put a few inches of damp sand in the aquarium first. It should be deep enough for your crabs to **burrow** in the sand. Then add freshwater, saltwater, and food into the tank.

Be sure to check the **humidity** level in the tank. It should be at least 70 percent for your crabs. You can find a special tool at the pet store to check this level.

Be careful with other animals in your home. Dogs or cats may try to eat hermit crabs.

burrow—a hole in the ground made or used by an animal; also, to dig
humidity—the measure of the moisture in the air

Many crabs sit in their water dishes, shell and all. You can use jar lids or clam shells as water bowls.

What Do Hermit Crabs Eat?

You can find hermit crab food at your pet supply store. Feed these **pellets** to your pets every day. You can also feed your crabs fresh fruits and vegetables.

Hermit crabs also eat meat. Most pet stores will have shrimp to feed your crabs. **Cuttlebones** are also good for hermit crabs. They are the insides of cuttlefish.

Some fruits that you can feed your crabs are coconuts, mangoes, and strawberries.

pellet—a small, hard piece of food; pellets give animals the nutrition they need

cuttlebone—the rough, oval-shaped bone of a cuttlefish

Cleaning Up

You will need to clean the food and water dishes every day. When you do this, remove any uneaten food from the tank.

Change the sand in the tank every few months. Place your crabs in a smaller tank while you clean. Before you add the fresh sand, wash the tank with hot water. Check the humidity level before adding your crabs back into the tank.

You do not need to wash your hermit crabs. They will clean themselves in the water you give them.

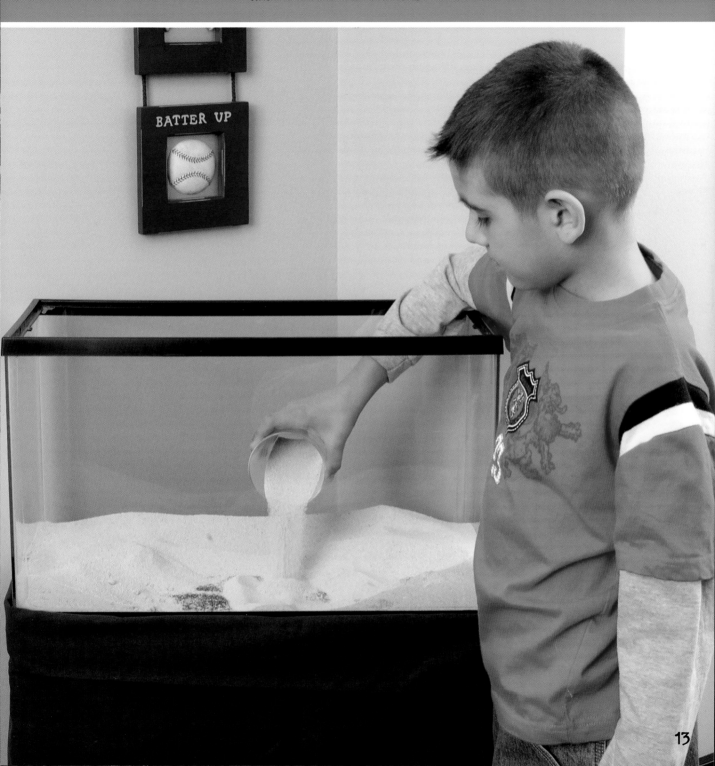

Taking Care of Hermit Crabs

Hermit crabs may move slowly or eat less sometimes. In most cases this just means that your pets are getting ready to **molt**. Hermit crabs shed their skin about once a year.

They also burrow for long periods. If your crabs stay under the sand for more than four weeks, call a **veterinarian**.

molt—to shed an outer layer of skin; after molting, a new covering grows

veterinarian—a doctor trained to take care of animals

FACT

A molting crab may seek out a dark spot in the tank. Add a small hut to the tank to give crabs a place to hide.

Life with Hermit Crabs

Place the tank in a warm, quiet spot. The tank should be 72 to 80 degrees Fahrenheit (22 to 27 degrees Celsius). Keep the tank away from heating or cooling vents.

You can take your pets out of their tanks for short amounts of time. Keep them safe on a smooth floor. Hermit crabs can catch their claws on carpeting.

FACT

Always pick up your crab by the back of its shell. This will help keep the crab from pinching you.

Hermit Crabs Through the Years

Do not dig up your crabs if they burrow for a long time. This is how hermit crabs stay calm.

If you take good care of your crabs, they will live for a long time. These animals have a **life span** of between six and 15 years.

life span—the number of years a certain kind
of plant or animal usually lives

Hermit Crab Body Language

A hermit crab is more likely to pinch when you first bring it home. This is often because it is hungry. It is hoping to grab onto food. Give your crab a few days to get used to its new home before picking it up. You may also want to give it some extra food during this time.

Types of Hermit Crabs

Common hermit crabs sold
in the United States:

- Caribbean crab
- Ecuadorian crab
- Ruggie
- Strawberry hermit crab

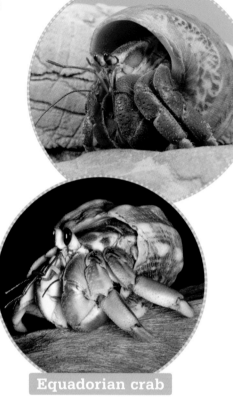

Caribbean crab

Equadorian crab

Ruggie

Strawberry crab

21

Glossary

aquarium (uh-KWAYR-ee-uhm)—a glass tank where pets, including hamsters, hermit crabs, and fish, are kept

burrow (BURH-oh)—a hole in the ground made or used by an animal; also, to dig

cuttlebone (KUHT-l-bohn)—the rough, oval-shaped bone of a cuttlefish

humidity (hyoo-MIH-du-tee)—the measure of the moisture in the air

life span (LIFE span)—the number of years a certain kind of plant or animal usually lives

molt (MOHLT)—to shed an outer layer of skin; after molting, a new covering grows

pellet (PEL-it)—a small, hard piece of food; pellets give animals the nutrition they need

thermometer (thur-MOM-uh-tur)—a tool that measures temperature

veterinarian (vet-ur-uh-NER-ee-uhn)—a doctor trained to take care of animals

Read More

Black, Vanessa. *Hermit Crabs.* My First Pet. Minneapolis: Jump!, Inc., 2017.

Murray, Julie. *Hermit Crabs.* Family Pets. Minneapolis: ABDO Kids, 2016.

Wittrock, Jeni. *Pet Hermit Crabs Up Close.* Pets Up Close. North Mankato, Minn.: Capstone Press, 2015.

Internet Sites

Use FactHound to find Internet sites related to this book.

Visit *www.facthound.com*

Just type in 9781543527421 and go.

Check out projects, games and lots more at
www.capstonekids.com

Critical Thinking Questions

1. Why is it important to have extra shells in the tank?

2. What are some of the foods that you can feed your hermit crabs?

3. What happens when a hermit crab is molting?

Index